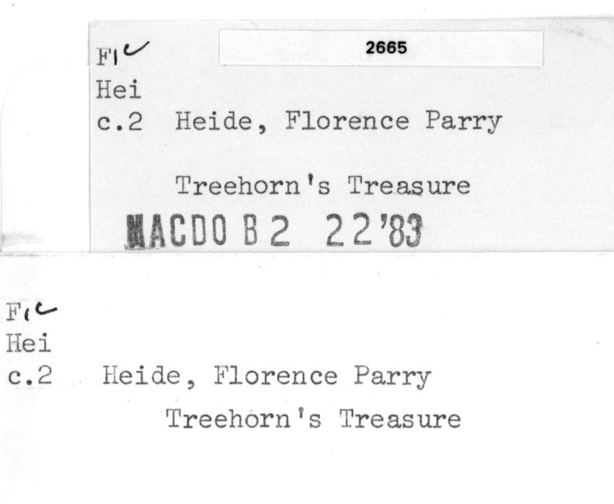

FLORENCE PARRY HEIDE

Treehorn's Treasure

DRAWINGS BY EDWARD GOREY

Holiday House New York

Printed in the United States of America
First Edition

Library of Congress Cataloging in Publication Data

Heide, Florence Parry.
Treehorn's treasure.

Summary: For one brief day the leaves of the maple tree in Treehorn's backyard turn into dollar bills.
[1. Money–Fiction] I. Gorey, Edward, 1925–
II. Title.
PZ7.H36Tr [Fic] 81-4043
ISBN 0-8234-0425-0 AACR2

For David Fisher Parry, my brother,
and his wife Jeanne, with love

Treehorn was sitting on his closet floor reading comic books. He had fourteen comic books and he had read each one nineteen times.

GULP! I'VE CUT OFF HIS HORRIBLE HEAD
AND LOOK! SHUDDER! HE'S GROWING ANOTHER
ONE! GASP! AND IT'S EVEN MORE HIDEOUS THAN
THE ONE I CUT OFF! UGH! YECCCH!

When Treehorn had finished reading that one, he put it on the bottom of the pile of comic books. The next one on the pile was THE VAMPIRE OF VILE VILLA. He hadn't read that one since the day before yesterday.

As soon as he got his allowance he could get some more. And he could send in for some of the things that were advertised in the comic books. He had the coupons all filled out and the envelopes all addressed and stamped. Maybe he could get his allowance this morning. He'd keep the envelopes in his raincoat pockets, just in case.

GLERRLOOK!

Treehorn put his raincoat on. Not because it was raining, because it wasn't, but because it had so many pockets. That way he could keep everything he needed right with him: comic books, and a flashlight, and some string and rubber bands and paper clips and small empty boxes, and some other things he might need.

His father was still at home having breakfast. "We're going to have to be more careful about what we spend, Emily," said Treehorn's father. "We're going to have to learn to save, save for a rainy day."

Treehorn's mother was draping different pieces of material over the furniture.

"Oh, I do hope it doesn't rain," she said. "I just had my hair done yesterday." She held up some of the material. "Do you like the stripe or the floral, Chester?"

"They're both very nice, dear," said Treehorn's father.

"Can I have my allowance?" asked Treehorn. "You forgot it last week so you owe me for two weeks."

"The painter's coming this morning to paint the kitchen," said Treehorn's mother. "As long as we're doing the kitchen, wouldn't it be nice to do the whole house?"

"Money doesn't grow on trees, Emily," said Treehorn's father.

"Well, at least I can do the chair over," sighed Treehorn's mother. "Maybe this nice nubby tweed. Green's very good this year. Eat your prunes, Treehorn."

PUFF, PUFF! I CAN'T RUN ANY FARTHER!
AND HE'S COMING CLOSER! COUGH! COUGH!
HE'S BREATHING FIRE! I'LL BE BURNED ALIVE!
GASP! CHOKE! IF ONLY I CAN MAKE IT TO THE RIVER! SPLASH! GLUG!

"I do wish Aunt Bertha wasn't coming for dinner tonight," said Treehorn's mother. "We'll just have to take her out, what with the painting and all."

"Well, let's not go anywhere expensive, Emily," said Treehorn's father. "Our money just seems to dribble away."

MPF!

The doorbell rang. "Oh dear, it's the painter already," said Treehorn's mother, going to answer the door.

"Can I have my allowance?" Treehorn asked his father. Treehorn's father looked at Treehorn. "There's something I wanted to talk to you about, Treehorn, but I've forgotten what it was."

"My allowance," said Treehorn. "You owe me for two weeks."

"It had something to do with money," said Treehorn's father.

"If I get it today I can send in for things," said Treehorn.

"I've just thought of what it was I wanted to talk to you about, Treehorn," said his father. "I have a surprise for you. I'm going to give you a whole dollar."

"You owe me for two weeks," said Treehorn.

"I'm going to give you a whole dollar," Treehorn's father went on. "And I want you to save it."

"If I save it I can't spend it," said Treehorn.

"That's the point, Treehorn. The whole purpose of money is to save. Save, not spend. A dollar saved is a dollar earned," said Treehorn's father. "A man's savings is a man's treasure."

"What good does it do if I just save it?" asked Treehorn. "I want to send in for things."

"Money doesn't grow on trees, Treehorn," said his father. "Put this dollar in a safe place. You'll be glad you did."

The safest place Treehorn could think of was his piggy bank, but his mother had put everything in the kitchen into boxes.

Another safe place was the hole in the tree in the yard. No one ever looked there. He could put the dollar in one of his envelopes and put the envelope in the hole. That should be pretty safe.

Treehorn took some of the envelopes he had addressed from his raincoat pockets. One of them was addressed to THE HE-MAN COMPANY. He had been going to send in for a strong-man kit like the one his friend Moshie had.

Another one was addressed to:

INSTANT MAGIC
BOX 11
N.Y., N.Y.

The coupon said:

VALUABLE COUPON!

SIMPLY SEND THIS COUPON
(plus one dollar)
LEARN! INCREDIBLE MAGIC FEATS!
ASTOUND YOUR FRIENDS!
STUPEFY YOUR FAMILY!
HURRY!
SUPPLY LIMITED!

Treehorn put the dollar bill in that envelope and went outside.

He had left yesterday's bubble gum in the hole in the tree, so he took it out and put in the envelope with the dollar instead. Then he sat down and leaned against the tree. He read a comic book and chewed his bubble gum.

He looked at the back cover after he had read the comic book three times.

NEXT ISSUE! THE MUMMY'S CURSE!

MIND BOGGLING HORROR!

BLOOD CURDLING TERROR!

SPINE TINGLING, NERVE SHATTERING SUSPENSE!

DON'T MISS THE MUMMY'S CURSE!

Treehorn was just getting comfortable when he looked up at the tree.

The leaves looked different. He stood up and looked more closely. He couldn't be sure, but it looked as though the leaves were turning into dollar bills. Not all of them, but some.

He'd have to get a ladder if he was going to pick any of them.

He went into the kitchen. His mother was talking to the painter.

"You've got the green all wrong," said Treehorn's mother to the painter. "It's supposed to be Leaf Green. That isn't Leaf Green."

"It's a nice green though," said the painter. "You have to admit it's a nice green."

"The leaves on the tree are all changing to dollar bills," said Treehorn.

"It's such a lovely day, dear, you should be playing outside," said Treehorn's mother.

"I am playing outside," said Treehorn. "I just came in to get a ladder. Can I borrow your ladder?" he asked the painter. "The leaves on that tree are all changing into dollar bills."

"Look," said the painter. "I got troubles of my own. And now your mother complains about my green, and you complain about your tree. I could tell you troubles that would make you cry."

"Well, can I borrow your ladder?" asked Treehorn.

"Sure," said the painter, "as long as I get it back."

Treehorn carried the ladder to the back door. His mother was sweeping the back steps.

"What are you doing with a ladder?" she asked.

"Some of the leaves of that tree are turning into dollar bills," said Treehorn. "I'm going to climb up and pick some."

"You know how your father feels about your climbing up on ladders," said Treehorn's mother. "Be very, very careful."

Treehorn put the ladder up beside the tree. He climbed up and looked at the leaves.

Lots of the dollars were ready. He picked twenty-six. There were a lot of others that were turning, but they weren't quite done yet. He could come back later and get those.

He took the ladder back into the kitchen.

"Look," said Treehorn to the painter. "I told you the leaves were turning into dollar bills."

The painter sighed. "In my day a kid had to work for his money. If you ask me, kids these days are spoiled rotten."

Treehorn put the dollars in his raincoat pockets. Then he walked to the neighborhood drugstore to get some new comic books.

He walked over to the comic book rack and picked out one copy of every one they had. They didn't have THE MUMMY'S CURSE, but they had a lot of other good ones. He would still have enough money left over to get some bubble gum.

There was one kind of bubble gum that came with pictures of baseball players. Treehorn would have bought that kind anyway, because it was BIGGER BUBBLE ("A Bigger Bubble Every Time"), but it was nice to have the pictures of the baseball players, too, even though Treehorn didn't like baseball very much.

He still had some money left over, so he picked out twenty-three candy bars and sixteen bottles of pop.

"Hey," said the girl behind the counter. "You must be having a party or something. You got enough money to pay for all this?"

"Yes," said Treehorn, counting out his money. "And I'm going to be having a lot more. The leaves on the tree in our yard are turning into dollar bills."

"Some people have all the luck," said the girl.

Treehorn thought he might have to make two trips, but he finally managed, what with his raincoat pockets and everything.

He carried his things upstairs. He put all of the new comic books on top of the pile in his closet, and the pile of bubble gum with baseball pictures in a pile right next to that pile. As soon as some more dollar bills were ripe, he could have a pile of those. He'd never had a pile of dollar bills. He'd had piles of play money, but that wasn't the same thing.

He put the pop bottles in a line all around the closet and the candy bars in a pile on his closet shelf. Then he read the comic book that was on the top of the pile of comic books.

He'd go out and check the tree later. Now he just wanted to read some of his new comic books.

BAM! BIFF! SPLASH!

JUST BECAUSE YOU'VE PUSHED ME INTO THIS VAT OF BOILING OIL, DOCTOR NONONO, IT DOESN'T MEAN YOU'VE SEEN THE LAST OF ME! I'M WEARING MY INVISIBLE WET SUIT!

“Come down and say hello to Aunt Bertha, Treehorn,” called Treehorn’s mother.

Aunt Bertha looked very much like Treehorn’s father, thought Treehorn, except that she didn’t have a moustache.

“So this is Treehorn,” said Aunt Bertha. “Looks just like poor Uncle Ferd.”

“Say hello to Aunt Bertha, Treehorn,” said Treehorn’s mother.

“What are you going to be when you grow up, Treehorn?” asked Aunt Bertha.

“We thought we’d have him go into banking,” said Treehorn’s mother.

Aunt Bertha nodded. “Banking is very nice. You always know where you stand in a bank.”

Treehorn thought maybe be should go outside now to look at the tree.

"Do you have any hobbies, Treehorn?" asked Aunt Bertha.

"Oh, Treehorn has lots of hobbies, don't you, Treehorn?" said Treehorn's mother.

"I like a boy who has hobbies," said Aunt Bertha. "All work and no play makes Jack a dull boy."

The telephone rang. Treehorn went into the hall to answer it. It was Treehorn's friend Moshie.

"What a boring summer," said Moshie. "And now school's going to start again. And *it's* going to be boring." Moshie yawned on the telephone. Moshie yawned a lot. "Did you write your book report yet?"

Treehorn was going to write his book report on THE HEADLESS HORROR. The teacher hadn't *said* they could write a book report on a comic book, but she hadn't said they *couldn't,* either.

"I haven't written it yet," said Treehorn.

"Me neither," said Moshie.

"The leaves on our tree are turning into dollar bills, so I picked some and bought a lot of new comic books," said Treehorn.

"Did you get THE MUMMY'S CURSE?" asked Moshie.

"They didn't have it," said Treehorn.

"I'll trade you ten baseball cards for it," said Moshie.

"I don't have it," said Treehorn.

"I'll throw in two of my best marbles," said Moshie.

"I didn't get it," said Treehorn.

"Some friend you are," said Moshie, and hung up.

Treehorn walked back into the living room.

"Of course it isn't any of my business, Emily, but Treehorn does look a little peaked," said Aunt Bertha. "Poor color."

"Yes, Treehorn," said Treehorn's mother. "You should be playing outside."

"I'm going outside now," said Treehorn. "The leaves on the tree are turning into dollar bills. I already picked twenty-six. If they're ripe I'm going to pick some more."

"I like a boy who likes nature," said Aunt Bertha. "Uncle Ferd liked nature. He could tell every kind of tree in the world just by looking at its leaf. In the world, mind you," said Aunt Bertha. "Can you do that, Treehorn?"

"I thought it was a maple tree, but now that the leaves are turning into dollar bills, I'm not sure," said Treehorn.

"Uncle Ferd was *always* sure," said Aunt Bertha. "If a thing's worth knowing, it's worth knowing well, he used to say. You'll have to read up on things, Treehorn. Uncle Ferd always read up on things."

"Oh, Treehorn is always reading," said Treehorn's mother.

The telephone rang again. Treehorn started out to the hall to answer it.

"Seems to have a head on his shoulders," said Aunt Bertha. Treehorn glanced in the mirror as he walked out of the room, but he didn't notice anything different.

"Hello, Emily," said Treehorn's father on the telephone.

"This is Treehorn," said Treehorn.

"We'll have to talk about Treehorn another time, Emily," said Treehorn's father. "I just called to tell you I won't be able to go with you tonight to dinner. I'm sorry to have to miss Aunt Bertha's visit, of course, but business is business."

"This is Treehorn," said Treehorn. "And the leaves on the tree are turning into dollar bills."

"Emily, we'll talk about money another time," said Treehorn's father.

"This is Treehorn," said Treehorn.

"Well, Treehorn, why didn't you say so?" said Treehorn's father. "Just tell you mother I won't be home for dinner."

Treehorn walked back into the living room.

"Of course it's none of my business, Emily," Aunt Bertha was saying, "but the green floral is absolutely dreadful. Of course if you like it, go right ahead."

Treehorn told his mother that his father wasn't coming home for dinner. Then he said, "I'm going back outside to see if any more leaves have turned into dollar bills."

Treehorn went out to look at the tree.

Every single one of the leaves was turning into a dollar bill. But they weren't quite done yet.

He sat down to wait. He took out one of his new comic books.

BANG! BANG!

LOOK! THE BULLETS ARE BOUNCING RIGHT OFF HIM! NOTHING CAN STOP HIM NOW—NOTHING!

Treehorn looked up at the leaves every now and then. They were almost ready to pick.

Treehorn's mother called him. "Treehorn, do come in. You're going to catch cold out there."

ANG!
NG!

Treehorn went inside. His mother said, "We're going out to have dinner at a lovely restaurant with Aunt Bertha, Treehorn. Be sure to wear the nice tie she gave you last Christmas."

Treehorn went upstairs to find the tie. He remembered the tie, partly because he had been very sorry at the time that it was a tie and not something else, and partly because he had just seen it somewhere. He couldn't remember where, but he'd just seen it. He knew that.

When he went into his closet to get a candy bar, he remembered. It was on the light cord. He'd tied it here a long time ago to make it easier to turn the light on and off. It was pretty wrinkled, but he could sit on it for a while and it would look all right. He climbed up to untie it. By the time he had read three more comic books the tie was ready and it was time to go.

It was very dark at the restaurant.

"Check your coats?" asked the hatcheck girl. Aunt Bertha and Treehorn's mother checked their coats. Treehorn decided to keep his raincoat on.

A man came up to them. "Two, madam? This way, please."

Treehorn followed his mother and Aunt Bertha. It was hard to see where they were going. The man led them to a table. Aunt Bertha and Treehorn's mother sat with their backs against the wall. The man handed them both a big black menu. There wasn't anywhere for Treehorn to sit, so he stood up.

"Oh dear," said Aunt Bertha. "I left my glasses in my coat."

"Oh, Treehorn will be glad to get them for you, won't you, Treehorn?" said Treehorn's mother. "Just ask the hatcheck girl in the lobby."

Treehorn started back to the lobby. He was glad he'd brought his flashlight.

Escuro's
Escuro's

When he had found his way back, the girl asked, "Check your coat, sir?"

Treehorn shook his head. "Guess what?" he asked. "The leaves on the tree in our backyard are turning into dollar bills."

The girl smiled. "My mother says that when I was a kid I pretended there was a pony in the backyard," she said.

"But the leaves really are turning into dollar bills," said Treehorn.

"She says I used to take breakfast out to it," said the girl.

Treehorn sighed. "Could I get my Aunt's glasses out of her coat?" he asked.

"You need a claim check for that," said the girl.

It was hard for Treehorn to find the right table because everyone was reading menus. He walked around with his flashlight until he heard Aunt Bertha's voice.

"I have to have the claim check or I can't get your glasses," said Treehorn.

"That's using your head, Treehorn," said Aunt Bertha. "I like a boy who uses his head." She reached in her purse and handed him the claim check.

"Isn't this a lovely dinner, Treehorn?" asked his mother.

Treehorn started back to the checkroom.

Escuro's
Escuro's

When he got there, the girl was talking with someone.

Treehorn stood there for a while, waiting for them to stop talking. Then he sat down and read MAXI MONSTER FROM OUTER SPACE. He read it four times.

When the girl was through talking he gave her the claim check and got the glasses.

Then he walked back to the table.

"Wasn't this a delicious dinner, Treehorn?" asked his mother.

Treehorn unwrapped another piece of bubble gum. He wished he'd brought one of his candy bars.

Escuro's

Aunt Bertha said goodbye when they got back to the house. "Not many boys your age are lucky enough to have dinner in a restaurant like that, Treehorn. Your little friends will be green with envy when they hear about it."

After she had left, Treehorn started outside with his flashlight. It wasn't as dark as it had been at the restaurant, but it was pretty dark.

"Where are you going, Treehorn?" asked his mother.

"I'm just going out to see if all the leaves on the tree have finished changing into dollar bills," said Treehorn. "They weren't quite done enough before."

"You know your father doesn't like you to go outside after dark, Treehorn," said his mother. "You'll have to wait until tomorrow morning."

Treehorn was going to see if there was something to eat in the refrigerator, but the boxes were piled in front of it. He was glad he had all those candy bars in his closet.

He went upstairs to his closet and tied the tie back on to the light cord. He read four more comic books and ate six candy bars before he went to bed.

The next morning when Treehorn came downstairs his father was having breakfast.

"I've been thinking about that dollar, Treehorn," he said. "I'm going to put it into a savings account for you. Remember, a man's savings is a man's treasure. That way you can see your money grow. There's nothing more satisfying than seeing money grow, Treehorn."

"I know," said Treehorn. "It's growing on the tree out in the yard. I'm just going out to pick some."

"Not many boys your age have a savings account," said Treehorn's father. "You get the dollar and I'll take it to the bank. You're never too young to start to save."

Treehorn went outside to get the dollar bill out of the hole in the tree. He looked up at the leaves. Every single one of them was ripe. There were hundreds and hundreds of dollar bills. Maybe thousands and thousands. Treehorn wondered if he would have enough room in his closet for all of them.

He could send for that book about magic this morning. There would be lots of things he could send for now. The strong-man kit, for instance. He could even send for two strong-man kits. He could send for two *hundred* if he wanted to.

He took the envelope addressed to INSTANT MAGIC from the hole in the tree. Then he took the dollar bill out of the envelope and took it in to his father.

“I’ve decided on the green floral,” said Treehorn’s mother.

“That’s nice, dear,” said Treehorn’s father.

Treehorn gave his father the dollar bill. Then he went out to the kitchen.

“Can I borrow your ladder again?” Treehorn asked the painter.

“Sure,” said the painter.

“All the leaves have turned into dollar bills,” said Treehorn. “There are hundreds and hundreds of dollar bills. I’m going out to pick them.”

“I still say a kid ought to work for his money,” said the painter.

Treehorn took the ladder and went outside. When he climbed up, he could see that all the dollar bills had started to fade. All that was left on the leaves were faces of George Washington, and they were fading, too.

Well, anyway, he still had all of those new comic books. It would take a long time to finish them. And by the time he got to the last one, maybe he'd have forgotten what the first ones were about and he could start all over again. Even if he hadn't forgotten what they were about he could read them over again.

He carried the ladder back to the kitchen.

"The dollar bills have all faded," Treehorn said to the painter. "They're all turning back into leaves."

"Everybody's got problems," said the painter.

Treehorn went upstairs to his closet. He wanted to see if the envelope addressed to THE HE-MAN COMPANY was still in his raincoat pocket. As soon as he got his next allowance, he'd send for that strong-man kit.